A SKATEBOARD CAT-ASTROPHE

Don't miss any of the cases in the Hardy Boys Clue Book series!

HARDY BOYS

→Clue Book←

#6

A SKATEBOARD CAT-ASTROPHE

BY FRANKLIN W. DIXON ⟿ ILLUSTRATED BY MATT DAVID

ALADDIN
NEW YORK   LONDON   TORONTO   SYDNEY   NEW DELHI

ALADDIN

An imprint of Simon & Schuster Children's Publishing Division
1230 Avenue of the Americas, New York, NY 10020
First Aladdin paperback edition November 2017
Text copyright © 2017 by Simon & Schuster, Inc.
Illustrations copyright © 2017 by Matt David
Also available in an Aladdin hardcover edition.
All rights reserved, including the right of reproduction in whole or in part in any form.
ALADDIN and related logo are registered trademarks of Simon & Schuster, Inc.
THE HARDY BOYS and colophons are registered trademarks of Simon & Schuster, Inc.
HARDY BOYS CLUE BOOK and colophons are trademarks of Simon & Schuster, Inc.
For information about special discounts for bulk purchases, please contact
Simon & Schuster Special Sales at 1-866-506-1949 or business@simonandschuster.com.
The Simon & Schuster Speakers Bureau can bring authors to your live event.
For more information or to book an event contact the Simon & Schuster Speakers Bureau
at 1-866-248-3049 or visit our website at www.simonspeakers.com.
Series designed by Karina Granda
Cover designed by Nina Simoneaux
The text of this book was set in Adobe Garamond Pro.
Manufactured in the United States of America 1019 OFF
4 6 8 10 9 7 5 3
Library of Congress Control Number 2016949156
ISBN 978-1-4814-8870-9 (hc)
ISBN 978-1-4814-8869-3 (pbk)
ISBN 978-1-4814-8871-6 (eBook)

CONTENTS

BATTLE OF THE BOARDS

"Wow!" eight-year-old Joe Hardy exclaimed. "Check out all the kids here to watch the skateboarders practice!"

Joe and his nine-year-old brother, Frank, gazed at the crowd gathered around the obstacle course. It had been set up in the park for the Bayport Skateboard Challenge in just two days.

"They're probably here to see Diesel Diffendorfer

practice," Frank figured. "He's Bayport's skateboard champ."

Their friend Chet Morton shook his head. "I think everyone's here for the Easy Cheesy Mac and Cheese truck," he said, "and their famous fried mac-and-cheese balls!"

The Easy Cheesy truck was parked a few feet away. The macaroni-and-cheese company was holding the skateboarding contest that Saturday.

"I heard the winner of the skateboard contest gets free mac and cheese the rest of the summer," Chet shared excitedly. "And summer just started!"

Frank and Joe traded grins. If Diesel was Bayport's champ skateboarder, Chet was Bayport's champion snacker!

"The winner also gets a gift card to the Complete Athlete store downtown," Frank added.

"Plus free skateboard lessons from a national pro!" Joe chimed in.

Chet thought for a moment, then shrugged and said, "Who needs that? Let's load up on mac and cheese!"

"Mac and cheese?" a girl's voice piped up. "Seriously?"

Frank, Joe, and Chet turned to see Daisy Zamora from school. Following Daisy were her six-year-old twin brothers Matty and Scotty.

The Zamoras owned the Pizza Palace restaurant on Bay Street, and Daisy never let anyone forget it.

"Did you ever see mac and cheese topped

with pepperoni, mushrooms, or peppers?" Daisy demanded. "Did you?"

"Uh . . . what's your point, Daisy?" Frank asked.

"Our pizzas taste way better than boring mac and cheese," Daisy said, handing each of them a coupon. "And today we're giving free toppings on all slices and pies."

"Nothing says yummy like pizza in your tummy!" Matty declared. "Scotty and I made that up."

"Plus," Daisy went on, "if you order any size pie, it will be delivered to your home with a free Pizza Palace Frisbee."

"A Frisbee, huh?" Joe said. "Thanks, Daisy, but we were just about to have some fried mac-and-cheese balls."

The twins' mouths dropped open.

"Fried mac-and-cheese balls?" Scotty exclaimed. "That's yummy for the tummy too!"

"Can we get some, Daisy?" Matty asked his sister. "Puh-leeeeeze?"

Daisy glared at her brothers. "If more and more kids eat macaroni and cheese," she said, "then our pizza place will go out of business."

"So?" Matty asked.

"So don't expect those new scooters you wanted!" Daisy snapped.

The twins stared, horrified, at Daisy, then at each other. They then hurried after Daisy to the next group of kids.

"Pizza Palace will never go out of business," Joe joked. "Not while Chet is around!"

"For sure," Chet agreed. "I may like mac and cheese, but pizza will always have my heart!"

The boys began walking toward the truck until a grinding noise stopped them in their tracks. Glancing back, they saw Diesel Diffendorfer carving his skateboard in their direction.

A tiny dog stood in Diesel's path. He jumped his skateboard over the dog, showed off with a kick-flip, then continued toward the Hardys and Chet.

"Hey!" Joe shouted as the three jumped to the side.

Diesel screeched to a stop, the nose of his board only inches away from Frank, Joe, and Chet. He popped his flame-painted skateboard out from under his feet.

"Oops," Diesel said, catching the board under one arm. "Sorry about that."

"Sorry?" Joe exclaimed. "You did that on purpose, Diesel, and you know it."

Diesel opened his mouth to speak as another voice called out, "Hardy, har, har!"

Frank and Joe traded eye rolls. They knew that laugh anywhere. It was nine-year-old Adam Ackerman, school bully and now best buds with Diesel!

"Where are your skateboards?" Adam sneered as he approached. "Oh wait, the contest probably doesn't allow training wheels."

"Very funny," Chet retorted. "Maybe Frank and Joe have better things to do—like being the best detectives in Bayport and maybe the world!"

"Second best in Bayport," Joe said with a smile. "Our dad is a private investigator."

As Joe spoke, he secretly placed a hand over the back pocket that held his clue book. The small notebook was where he and Frank wrote down all their clues and suspects. If Adam saw it, he would grab it for sure!

"Detectives!" Diesel scoffed. He twirled a wheel on his skateboard and said, "Who wants to be that when you can be skateboard king like me?"

"King?" Joe raised an eyebrow. "Or joker?"

In a flash Adam loomed over Joe. "I dare you to find a better skateboarder than Diesel, Hardy," he growled.

From the corner of his eye, Joe could see Frank and Chet coming to his rescue. Luckily, they didn't have to. . . .

"Hey, Diesel!" a voice shouted. "How about a selfie?"

Joe looked over Adam's shoulder to see three kids racing over. They all wore T-shirts reading, GO DIESEL!

"Hey, it's my fan club!" Diesel said excitedly. "Adam, dude, watch while I get totally worshipped."

Adam shot Joe one last glare, then left to join Diesel and the fans.

"A whole summer of Adam Ackerman," Joe groaned as they walked on to the mac-and-cheese truck. "Is it too late to go to camp?"

"I know a skateboarder who would wipe the floor with Diesel Diffendorfer," said Chet. "That would show Adam."

"Who's better than Diesel?" Frank asked.

Chet pulled a small computer tablet out of his backpack. He opened YouTube, then searched for a video of Skeeter the Skateboarding Cat.

"The skateboarder is a cat?" Frank asked, surprised.

"Our aunt Trudy started rescuing stray cats," Joe added. "By now she must have over a hundred in her apartment over our garage."

"You're going to wish your aunt Trudy rescued this cat!" Chet said. He held the tablet as the video played. "Watch and be amazed!"

Frank and Joe watched wide-eyed as the gray-and-white tabby cat ran his skateboard down a ramp and over a rail, then jumped obstacles like a pro!

"Wow!" Frank exclaimed.

"Skeeter is awesome!" Joe declared.

"Here's the best part," Chet said. "Skeeter's owner is named Carlos Martinez. He's nine, and his family just moved to Bayport."

"How do you know?" Frank asked.

"How else?" Chet asked with a grin. "Skeeter has his own website."

Joe scrunched his brow thoughtfully. "Martinez . . . Martinez," he said before looking at Frank. "Didn't Mom just sell a house to a family named Martinez?"

Frank nodded. Their mom, Laura Hardy, was a real estate agent in Bayport.

"Mom did say something about a kid named Carlos being in my grade in the fall," Frank said. "That must be him."

"So Skeeter must be his cat," Chet said excitedly.

Joe smiled. It was cool having a pet celebrity in their hometown. It was also cool to have a new kid around.

"Why don't we go over and say hi to Carlos?" Joe suggested. "He probably wants to make new friends."

"We can meet Skeeter, too," Chet said, then quickly added, "After mac and cheese!"

The boys lunched on fried mac-and-cheese balls and lemonade before leaving the park for the Martinez house.

"Are you sure this is where Carlos lives?" Chet asked after reaching Tidewater Street. "There's no name on the mailbox."

"Mom told us it was the only yellow house on this street," Frank said as they faced the yellow house with the green roof. "And this is it."

The boys started up the path to the front door. Joe was about to ring the bell when he heard a rumbling noise.

"What's that?" Joe asked.

"It sounds like it's coming from the backyard," Frank said. "Let's check it out."

The noise grew louder and louder as Frank, Joe, and Chet walked along the side of the house. When they reached the backyard, they couldn't believe their eyes. . . .

"Holy cannoli!" Joe exclaimed.

Set up in the Martinezes' backyard was an elaborate course of rails, ramps, and quarter pipes. Running a skateboard through the course was a gray-and-white cat!

"I think we're looking at Skeeter!" Frank said.

"I think we're looking at the next Bayport skateboarding champ!" Joe declared.

Two of Skeeter's paws were planted on the board

as it zoomed up and down a quarter pipe. The boys watched in awe as the cat spun his board around and around!

A boy wearing a T-shirt and shorts walked over to Frank, Joe, and Chet. "Pretty awesome, huh?" he asked.

"Totally!" Joe agreed. "I'll bet you're Carlos!"

"I'll bet you're right!" Carlos said with a grin.

Frank, Joe, and Chet introduced themselves. Skeeter needed no introduction.

"Have you seen Skeeter's videos?" Carlos asked.

"Your cat is a superstar," Joe said with a grin. "Isn't it time to make him a champion?"

"What do you mean?" said Carlos.

"Enter him in the Bayport Skateboard Challenge on Saturday," Chet chimed in excitedly.

Frank couldn't believe his ears. "Are you guys serious?" he asked Joe and Chet. "How do we know the contest even allows cats?"

"It will now!" Chet insisted. "Frank, a skate-boarding cat would be great publicity for the Easy Cheesy truck."

"Chet's right," Joe agreed. "The owner would be nuts to say no."

"I would be too," Carlos declared happily. "What a cool way to introduce Skeeter—and myself—to Bayport!"

Carlos turned to his cat and said, "What do you say, Skeeter?"

"Meeeeooowww!" Skeeter howled before jumping a patio chair and landing on his board.

"Diesel Diffendorfer," Joe declared, "you are about to meet your match!"

Chapter 2

KITTY BITTER

"I knew the Martinezes had a cat," Laura Hardy said as she chopped a stalk of celery into tiny pieces. "But I had no idea that he could skateboard!"

The Hardys were in the kitchen preparing dinner. Frank and Joe had just told their dad, mom, and Aunt Trudy all about Skeeter.

"He doesn't just skateboard, Mom," Joe explained. "This cat does extreme tricks!"

"That's pretty amazing," Fenton Hardy said.

"Really, Fenton?" Aunt Trudy scoffed as she filled the water pitcher. "I find it extremely disturbing."

"Why, Aunt Trudy?" Frank asked.

"You know how much I like cats," Aunt Trudy said, placing the pitcher on the counter with a *clunk*. "And cats should be cats."

When everyone looked confused, Aunt Trudy explained. "Cats weren't meant to ride skateboards. They were meant to sit on windowsills, watching the birds outside. They were meant to swat at butterflies—and chase mice!"

"Mice?" Mr. Hardy said as he pulled dishes from the kitchen cabinet. "I hope there aren't any mice in your apartment, Trudy!"

"How many cats have you rescued over the years, Aunt Trudy?" Joe asked. "Three hundred?"

Aunt Trudy chuckled. "You know, I'm not sure. Let's just say that a mouse hasn't had a chance in my apartment for a long time."

"Hey, look!" Frank said, pointing to the small TV on the counter. "There's Skeeter now!"

All eyes turned to the TV. On it was a local news

reporter interviewing Carlos Martinez. In Carlos's arms was Skeeter the cat!

"Now that Skeeter will be competing in the Bayport Skateboard Challenge, do you think he has a chance to win?" Kimberly Post, the reporter, asked Carlos.

"Skeeter didn't become a YouTube star by chasing his tail, Ms. Post," Carlos replied. "He can beat anyone."

"Even Diesel Diffendorfer?" Ms. Post probed. "Bayport's reigning champ?"

Before Carlos could answer, Chet stepped into the shot. "Diesel who?" he joked. He pointed at Skeeter with a fried mac-and-cheese ball. "The cat is out of the bag—and the prize will be in!"

Excited, Joe turned to Frank. "Chet made a deal with the Easy Cheesy truck to allow Skeeter in the contest!"

"You heard it right here, folks," Ms. Post declared.

"Skeeter the famous skateboarding cat will be competing in Bayport's Skateboard Challenge on Saturday. The contest begins at eleven o'clock sharp, so we'll see you there! This is Kimberly Post for WBAY-TV News."

Frank and Joe exchanged a big high five.

"Congratulations, guys," Fenton told them.

"Yes, very cool," Mrs. Hardy agreed. She turned to Aunt Trudy. "What dressing would you like on your salad, Trudy?"

Aunt Trudy's mouth was a grim line. "No dinner for me, Laura," she muttered.

"No dinner?" Fenton asked, about to carry the dishes to the dining room.

"Not tonight, Fenton," Aunt Trudy answered as she headed toward the door. "I'll eat upstairs in my apartment. With my cats."

Frank and Joe watched Aunt Trudy leave through the kitchen door.

"Uh-oh," Joe said with a frown. "I have a feeling Aunt Trudy isn't happy about Skeeter being in the contest."

"Aunt Trudy won't be the only one," Frank said. "Wait until Adam Ackerman finds out."

After dinner Frank and Joe tossed a Frisbee in the front yard. Thanks to summer, it was still light outside.

"Catch this one!" Joe told Frank as he hurled the Frisbee super high in the air.

"Piece of cake!" Frank shouted. He stretched his arm to catch the whizzing Frisbee. But before he could grab it—

"Woof!"

A bulldog zipped over. The brothers watched as the dog jumped sky-high before snatching the Frisbee between his teeth.

"Wow! Frank, isn't that Phil's dog, Champ?" Joe asked.

Phil Cohen, the brothers' friend, walked into the yard, carrying a leash. "I didn't name him Champ for nothing," he said.

Joe noticed that Phil wasn't smiling. "What's up, Phil?" he asked.

"I just heard that Skeeter the Skateboarding Cat is going to be in the contest on Saturday," Phil answered.

"That's great, isn't it?" Frank asked.

"This is great," Phil declared. He pulled out his phone, then played a YouTube video. It was a video of Champ jumping high in the air and spinning before catching a Frisbee.

"Cool, Phil," Joe said. "I knew Champ caught Frisbees, but I didn't know he could do all that!"

"Champ had over two thousand fans on YouTube," Phil explained. "But ever since tonight's news report, Skeeter the Skateboarding Cat has more fans than Champ!"

Champ lowered his head and whined.

"But that'll change soon," Phil said, flashing a smile. "Soon everyone in Bayport will know who the real pet celeb is, and it won't be Skeeter!"

As Phil led Champ out of the yard, he called over his shoulder, "Just wait. You'll see!"

"What do you think Phil meant when he said we'll see?" Frank asked when Phil was out of earshot.

Joe shrugged. "Maybe Champ skateboards too!"

Saturday morning the Hardys and Chet headed straight to Bayport Park, where they gathered with dozens of other kids for the Bayport Skateboard Challenge.

"It's only ten thirty and Easy Cheesy is already serving mac and cheese!" Joe said, looking at the café tables filled with hungry diners.

"Macaroni and cheese for breakfast?" Frank exclaimed. "Whatever happened to eggs and toast?"

"It's never too early for mac and cheese," Chet stated. "Or for pizza. Look, here comes Daisy with some samples."

Daisy Zamora walked over, holding a plate filled with garlic knots. "Pizza Palace is serving free garlic knots with every pizza purchase today!" she said.

Chet took a knot. Frank and Joe both said no thanks. If it was too early for mac and cheese, it was way too early for garlic knots.

"Where are your little brothers?" Frank asked.

"Off playing somewhere," Daisy answered. "I guess they got tired of working."

"I'll never get tired of these garlic knots!" Chet said before popping it into his mouth. "Mmm-mm!"

As Daisy walked away, the boys checked out the crowd. Lots of kids from the neighborhood were there. So was the news crew from Station WBAY-TV, ready to report on Skeeter!

"Diesel-mania is now Skeeter-mania!" Joe pointed out. "Even Diesel's fan club is wearing 'Go Skeeter' T-shirts."

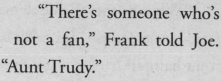

"There's someone who's not a fan," Frank told Joe. "Aunt Trudy."

Joe looked to see where Frank was pointing. Sure enough, there was Aunt Trudy, holding a sign that read, LET CATS BE CATS!

"There's only one cat I'm thinking about today, Frank," Joe insisted. "That's Skeeter!"

"Hey, Hardys!" an angry voice shouted.

Joe didn't have to look to know who it was. "Adam Ackerman," he muttered through gritted teeth.

Adam stormed over to Frank, Joe, and Chet. Right behind him were his equally bully-ish friends, Seth and Tony.

"I heard getting Skeeter in the contest was your idea," Adam snapped at Joe.

"What if it was?" Joe demanded.

"It was a dumb idea," Adam said angrily. "Because that hairball hacker is going down!"

"May the best skateboarder win, Adam," Frank said, "whether he has two legs—or four!"

Adam huffed off, Seth and Tony behind him.

"Who cares about them?" Chet said. "Because Skeeter is in the house!"

Chet pointed to Carlos in the distance, holding Skeeter. The celebrity cat was trying to lick its paws, as if he were getting ready for his big moment in the spotlight.

"There's the real champ!" Frank declared.

"I'm looking at you, Skeeter, dude!" Joe shouted to the cat. "Knock 'em off their wheelies!"

Skeeter's meow was followed by the crackle of the loudspeaker. It was an announcement from the owner of Easy Cheesy, Lou Simonetti.

"Before we begin the first annual Bayport Skateboard Challenge," Lou boomed, "let's give a big cheer for Easy Cheesy's awesome new outdoor space!"

While everyone cheered, Frank asked Joe, "Where did Aunt Trudy go?"

Joe didn't see her either. "Maybe to get some mac and cheese?" he guessed.

Lou introduced two judges seated at a table behind the skateboard course. They were Brad Lopez, a national skateboard champ, and Linda Blake, the owner of the Complete Athlete store. One more chair stood empty for the third judge, Lou himself.

Frank, Joe, and Chet listened to Lou describe the rules: contestants would be judged for skill, speed, and tricks. It was up to each skater whether to use the ramps, rails, or obstacles.

"So let the first annual Bayport Skateboard Challenge begin!" Lou declared.

Frank checked his watch. "Eleven o'clock, right on time," he said, impressed.

The first contestant was a middle schooler named Felicia Singh. Felicia skated from the ramp to the rail, wrapping up her routine with an awesomely high kick-flip.

"Go, Felicia!" Joe cheered along with the others. She was good, but wait until everyone saw Skeeter!

Next up was a boy from Frank's fourth-grade class. Marco Arroyo jumped every single obstacle before performing a coconut wheelie down the rest of the course.

"Cool," Joe said. "But I'll bet Skeeter can do all that."

"We're about to find out," Frank said.

Carlos carried Skeeter and his skateboard to the starting line. A team of cheerleaders waving pom-poms and wearing GO SKEETER T-shirts began to chant, "Two, four, six, eight—we think Skeeter's really great!"

With a meow, Skeeter hopped up on his board. Carlos gave his cat a thumbs-up, then stepped back. After a few seconds the starting bell rang. Skeeter was about to kick off when—*WHOOSH*—something small and gray with a long, skinny tail whizzed right by his skateboard.

"Is that a mouse?" Joe gasped.

Skeeter let out a loud *HISSSS*. He then leaped off his skateboard to chase the runaway rodent!

"This can't be good," Chet said.

Frank and Joe turned to look for Carlos. The first person they saw was Adam Ackerman, laughing it up. But then Carlos rushed forward, a frantic look on his face.

"Somebody get my cat!" Carlos cried as Skeeter chased the mouse into a thick clump of bushes. "Somebody get Skeeter!"

Chapter
3

CAT 'N' LOUSE

"We'll get him, Carlos!" Frank promised.

In a flash, he and Joe raced through the bushes after Skeeter. They found the cat in a clearing, the gray mouse between his paws.

Skeeter greeted them with a quiet "Meow."

"What's that whirring noise?" Frank asked.

"It's coming from the mouse," Joe said. "But it's not a mousy noise."

Skeeter didn't protest as Joe picked up the mouse. It was made out of metal!

"This thing is mechanical," Joe said. "That means someone ran it past Skeeter on purpose."

"We don't know for sure," Frank said. "But if somebody did do this, we'd better find out who."

The mouse stopped whirring in Joe's hand. "Let's do that later, Frank," he said. "Skeeter's still got a contest to win."

Frank carried the mouse out of the bushes while Joe carried Skeeter. As they returned to the skateboard course, another skater was wowing the crowd with fancy moves. It was Diesel Diffendorfer.

The brothers watched wide-eyed as Diesel performed an awesome Caballerial—a 360-degree turn on a ramp while riding backward!

Diesel rode his board off the ramp to thunderous applause. He pumped his fist in the air and took a bow.

"See, Hardy-har-hars?" Adam shouted. "When the cat's away, the real champ will win!"

Frank noticed Adam's smug expression. Did he

have something to do with the mechanical mouse? And where were Seth and Tony?

"Don't count your chickens before they hatch, Ackerman!" Joe shouted back. He lifted the cat in his arms. "Skeeter is back and better than ever."

"Not anymore," a sad voice said.

Frank and Joe turned to see Carlos, a frown on his face. "While you were in the bushes, the judges told me Skeeter is disqualified for running away."

"Disqualified?" Frank exclaimed.

"No way!" Joe protested.

The next skater zoomed onto the course while Carlos took Skeeter from Joe's arms.

"Not only was Skeeter disqualified," Carlos said sadly, "his reputation as a YouTube star is ruined!"

"It's not Skeeter's fault, Carlos," Joe said. "As our aunt Trudy says, cats are cats. And cats chase mice."

"Mechanical mice!" Frank said, lifting the fake mouse by its tail.

Carlos stared at the mouse. "You mean it's fake?" he asked. "Somebody did it on purpose?"

"Looks that way, Carlos," Frank admitted.

Carlos narrowed his eyes. "Then Bayport is the meanest town I ever lived in!" he said angrily.

"No, it's not," Frank said.

"It's got great people," Joe insisted. He glanced sideways at Adam and said, "Minus one or two."

"Well, now I hate it here," Carlos cried. "And I wish I'd never listened to you guys. I wish I'd never entered Skeeter in the contest!"

With his free hand, he picked up Skeeter's skateboard. The cat meowed as Carlos huffed away.

"Now Carlos hates Bayport," Frank sighed.

"That stinks," Joe said.

Chet walked over, sipping cold lemonade from an Easy Cheesy paper cup. "I heard what the judges told Carlos," he said. "Bummer."

Joe turned to the café tables in front of the Easy Cheesy truck. The once-filled tables were now empty.

"What happened to all the people?" Joe asked Chet. "The ones eating mac and cheese?"

"They saw the mouse and left," Chet said. "No one wants to eat at a place that has mice."

"But it was fake!" Joe said.

"Too late," Frank sighed. "The damage to the Easy Cheesy truck has been done."

"Oh, well," Chet said with a smile. "Fewer people equals more macaroni and cheese for us!"

Frank didn't feel like eating. Neither did Joe. Someone had run a fake mouse past Skeeter to get him out of the contest—and that someone had to be caught!

"No mac and cheese for us, Chet," Frank said. "Joe and I have work to do."

"Right!" Joe said as he pulled out his clue book. "Detective work!"

The brothers said good-bye to Chet and left the park, not staying to watch the rest of the contest. While Frank studied the mouse, Joe flipped to a clean page in his clue book.

"This mouse doesn't have buttons or a key," Frank pointed out. "How do you think it runs?"

"Probably with a remote control," Joe decided. "So whoever had the mouse still has the remote."

"And a reason for ruining Skeeter's chance in the

contest," Frank added. "Now we have to figure out who has the remote plus a motive."

Joe stopped walking to write the word *Suspects* at the top of the page. He immediately wrote the first name on the suspect list: *Adam Ackerman*.

"Adam wanted Skeeter out of the contest so Diesel could win," Joe said. "If you ask me, he's guilty as charged."

"Not so fast," Frank said. "Adam may have a reason—but we don't know if he has the remote."

The brothers continued walking. Joe smiled at the mouse in Frank's hand.

"Phil would love that thing," Joe declared. "He's got all kinds of gadgets and gizmos—"

"Phil!" Frank cut in.

"What about him?" said Joe.

"Remember how scared Phil was of Skeeter stealing Champ's spotlight?" Frank asked. "He also said we'd soon find out who the real Bayport celebrity pet was."

Frank narrowed his eyes thoughtfully. "And when Phil's not collecting gadgets, he's building his own!"

Joe knew what Frank meant. Phil was a gear nut and proud of it. But had Phil built the runaway mouse? Joe sure hoped not.

"We've been friends with Phil forever, Frank," he argued.

"Carlos is our new friend," Frank said. "We should help him find out who tricked Skeeter out of the contest."

"Wait, was Phil even at the contest?" Joe asked.

"I didn't see him, but if he was out to sabotage Skeeter, he wouldn't want too many people to see him," Frank said.

"I guess." Joe held the pen over his suspect list but still couldn't write Phil's name.

"Maybe we'll think of other suspects," he said, shutting his clue book and dropping it into his pocket.

When the brothers reached their house, the garage door was open.

"Let's go through the garage into the house," Frank suggested.

As they walked toward the garage, Frank noticed

something sticking out of the recycling bin against the side of the house. It was Aunt Trudy's protest sign, LET CATS BE CATS!

"Isn't it weird that Aunt Trudy left before the skateboard contest was over?" Frank asked.

When Frank lifted the sign to get a better look, he spotted something else in the can. It was a shopping bag from Marty's Meow Mart.

"Isn't Marty's Meow Mart the cat store on Bay Street?" Frank asked.

"It sure is," Joe tapped his foot and got a serious look on his face. "You don't think . . . ?"

"I don't think what? What are you looking for?" Frank asked as Joe rummaged through the bag.

"This." Joe pulled out a receipt.

Joe read the items on the receipt out loud: "Two sisal scratch pads, one kitty nail clipper, one Meandering Mechanical Mouse—"

"Mechanical mouse?" Frank interrupted.

"Uh-oh, I was afraid of this. . . ." Joe shuffled his feet.

Did the mechanical mouse that tricked Skeeter belong to Aunt Trudy?

Chapter 4

MEOW FACTOR

"Why would Aunt Trudy want to sabotage Skeeter?" Frank wondered. "That's not something she would do."

"Maybe she wanted to prove cats shouldn't be skateboarding," Joe suggested. "She did say cats should be chasing mice instead."

"I know," Frank agreed, "but how are we going to question our own aunt?"

"I have an idea," Joe said. "Let's just ask Aunt

Trudy about the mechanical mouse. It's probably a coincidence."

The brothers climbed the stairs up to Aunt Trudy's apartment over the garage.

Joe rapped four times on the door. When Aunt Trudy didn't answer, Frank said, "Maybe she's in the back. Knock louder."

Joe gave the door three strong raps. The third rap made it fly open.

"Oops," Joe said. "I guess she didn't close the door all the way."

"Aunt Trudy, are you home?" Frank called. There was no response, so the brothers stepped inside the apartment and called again. No answer.

"Where are her cats?" Frank asked, looking around the living room. "And where are all the cat toys?"

Joe didn't see any evidence of cats either. But he did see a cardboard box on the coffee table. . . .

"Frank!" Joe exclaimed. "It's the box for the Meandering Mechanical Mouse!"

He shook the box, then peeked inside. "It's

empty," he declared. "Which means Aunt Trudy probably used it."

Frank compared their mouse to the one on the box. "The mouse on the box is battery operated," he told his brother. "Ours runs by remote control."

"The Meandering Mouse has a cartoony face," said Joe, pointing to the box. "The one Skeeter chased looks real."

"Then where is the Meandering Mouse?" Frank asked. "And Aunt Trudy's rescue cats?"

Suddenly—*WHIRRRRRR* . . .

"It sounds like it's coming from Aunt Trudy's bedroom," Frank said, looking at the closed door.

"Maybe Aunt Trudy left her TV on when she went to the contest," Joe figured. "Let's turn it off for her."

He pushed open the door, then jumped as a whirring mechanical mouse zipped out. It was the Meandering Mechanical Mouse—followed by a stampede of cats!

"Noooo!" Frank shouted as meowing cats chased the mechanical mouse around the room, knocking

down books, sofa pillows—even a glass vase he caught just in time.

"You know what, Frank? " Joe cried, trying to keep a cat from climbing the drapes. "I think Aunt Trudy has too many cats!"

As the Meandering Mouse zipped between Joe's legs, a voice shouted, "Oh, my goodness! Oh, my goodness!"

The brothers spun around. Standing in the door way was Aunt Trudy.

"Frank, Joe?" Aunt Trudy demanded. "What on earth is going on in here?"

Chapter 5

SLICK TRICK

"Um . . . hi, Aunt Trudy," Joe said.

"Did you let my cats out of my bedroom?" Aunt Trudy asked. "I keep them in there when I go out so they don't run wild through the apartment . . . like they just did."

"Sorry, Aunt Trudy," Frank said. He pointed to the Meandering Mouse box now on the floor. "We were just looking for that."

"And we found it," Joe sighed as the Meandering

Mechanical Mouse shot head-on into the wall with a *BUMP*. "Plus your two hundred cats."

"Eight cats, actually," Aunt Trudy said, now smiling.

She went into the kitchen and came out carrying a big bag of kitty treats. Shaking it, she led all the cats into the bedroom, where she filled several bowls.

"There!" Aunt Trudy said, closing the door on her way out. "Those kitties will be too busy snacking to make any more mischief."

Then she turned to the mechanical mouse. "So, why were you looking for that mouse, guys?" she asked.

Joe explained everything: how they'd seen her at the skateboard contest, how Skeeter had been disqualified for chasing a fake mouse, and finally, how they'd found the receipt.

"We know you didn't like the idea of a skateboarding cat, Aunt Trudy," Frank admitted. "So we wondered if the runaway mouse was yours."

"Of course not! I still don't really like the idea of

cats on skateboards," Aunt Trudy replied. "But then I saw how happy Skeeter looked at the contest. I also saw how many people loved him."

"So," Joe said slowly. "You—"

"Changed my mind," Aunt Trudy finished. "I decided if skateboarding makes some cats happy, then I'm happy too."

"Did you stay to watch Skeeter?" Frank asked. "We didn't see you when the contest started."

"No, I left early. I decided to make my own rescue cats happy," Aunt Trudy explained. "So I went straight to Marty's Meow Mart for something fun they could play with."

"The Meandering Mechanical Mouse!" Joe confirmed.

"As I said, cats should be chasing mice," Aunt Trudy said with a smile, "even if they are fake."

As they helped their aunt clean up the mess, Frank and Joe whispered back and forth.

"I know Aunt Trudy wouldn't lie to us, Frank," Joe said. "But how do we know she really left when she says she did?"

Frank wasn't sure either until he figured out a way to check Aunt Trudy's alibi. "Give me the receipt," he told Joe.

Frank studied the receipt and said, "The time on the receipt is eleven thirty. Skeeter's turn came at eleven fifteen."

"How do you know it was eleven fifteen?" Joe asked.

"The contest started at eleven," Frank explained. "There were two skaters before Skeeter, and each had five minutes to run their skateboards."

"So with a few minutes in between each skater," Joe said out loud, "by the time Skeeter went, it could have been about eleven fifteen!"

"It takes about twenty minutes to walk from the park to Marty's Meow Mart," Frank went on. "So if Aunt Trudy was already buying the mouse at eleven thirty—"

"She would have left the park before Skeeter competed," Joe cut in. "Aunt Trudy's alibi checks out!"

Aunt Trudy was too busy picking up knocked-down sofa pillows to notice the boys whispering.

"Boys, don't tell your mom and dad what happened," she said. "Or they'll never let you get a cat!"

"They make mechanical mice," Joe said with a grin. "Maybe they make mechanical cats, too."

He and Frank finished cleaning up the rest of the mess. Aunt Trudy thanked them with some chocolate brownies and lemonade.

"I told you Aunt Trudy would never lie to us," Joe told Frank as they walked down the stairs. They were heading for the house when they saw Chet standing on the doorstep.

"I was just about to ring your bell," their friend said as he studied Joe's face. "Are those brownie crumbs on your chin? Where did you get them? Tell me!"

"Chet!" Joe sighed, rubbing the crumbs off his chin. "When don't you think of food?"

"When I'm sleeping," Chet replied. "Unless dreaming about food counts."

His face suddenly became superserious. "Anyway, I'm here because Adam and his friends took over the tables outside the Easy Cheesy café truck."

"What do you mean?" Frank asked.

"They're celebrating Diesel's big win at the skateboarding contest," Chet explained. "He scored first prize and free mac and cheese for a whole year."

"Diesel won?" Frank asked with a frown.

"Bummer," Joe sighed.

"Adam, Seth, and Tony are already giving Easy Cheesy a bad name," Chet said angrily. "Worse than that runaway mouse!"

Joe turned to Frank and said, "I think our next stop will be Easy Cheesy."

"For cheese balls?" Chet asked hopefully.

"For goofballs," Joe replied. "Adam Ackerman and his bully friends."

"Good idea," Frank said. "If Adam ran the mouse past Skeeter, then he's got to have the remote."

The brothers and Chet headed to the park and the Easy Cheesy truck. Adam, Seth, Tony, and Diesel were yukking it up around a café table. Diesel's skateboard was parked near his feet.

"Let's get closer," Frank whispered.

The boys ducked behind a tree. They then flitted

from tree to tree until they were only a few feet away from the bullies' table. Carefully Frank, Joe, and Chet peeked out.

"Something silver with buttons is on the table," Joe whispered. "It could be the remote!"

The boys leaned forward, listening in.

"My skateboard never went so fast, dudes," Diesel was saying. "No wonder I won the big kahuna of a prize!"

"You won because my trick worked!" Adam insisted. "And because no one saw Seth hiding with the remote."

All three boys traded looks. Trick? Remote? Bingo!

"That's got to be the remote for the mouse," Frank whispered. "We've got to get our hands on it."

"I know, Frank," Joe whispered. "There's just one problem."

"What?" Frank and Chet hissed.

"If we get our hands on the remote," Joe whispered, "Adam, Seth, and Tony will get their hands on us!"

Chapter 6

SQUEALS ON WHEELS

Frank, Joe, and Chet silently watched Adam and his friends. How could they check out the remote with them sitting right there? Things looked hopeless until the sound of bells filled the air.

"Hey, you guys!" Adam exclaimed, jumping up from his seat. "It's the ice-cream cart!"

"Awesome!" Diesel exclaimed, jumping up too. "I want a coconut crunch bar!"

"I want a fudge pop!" Seth said.

"Ice-cream sandwich all the way!" Tony declared.

The brothers and Chet ducked behind the tree as the bullies charged toward the ice-cream cart parked in the distance.

"Some tough guys!" Joe scoffed. "They're running for ice cream like a bunch of little kids!"

"Dude. We ran after an ice-cream truck, like, yesterday," Chet reminded him.

"While they're away from the table, let's run for that remote," Frank said.

"You guys do that," Chet said as they walked out from behind the tree. "I'm checking out the cheese dip they left on the table!"

The cheese dip wasn't all they'd left.

"Chet, what are you doing?" Frank asked as his friend hopped up on the skateboard.

"Hey, look, you guys!" Chet cheered. "I'm standing on the champ's skateboard!"

Frank and Joe were too busy examining the remote to pay attention to Chet.

"It looks like a remote," Frank pointed out. "But does it work with the mouse?"

There was only one way to find out. Joe pulled the mechanical mouse from his pocket. He placed it on the table and said, "Press the green button, Frank."

But when Frank pressed the button, the mouse didn't move. Instead—

"Ahhhhh!" Chet screamed.

Frank and Joe turned, their mouths dropping open. The skateboard with Chet was barreling forward at top speed!

"That's Diesel's board, Chet!" Joe shouted. "Stop!"

"I can't!" Chet yelled. "It's moving on its own!"

Frank stared at the remote in his hand. "Joe," he gulped. "This remote doesn't operate the mouse. It operates Diesel's skateboard!"

The brothers raced after Chet, pressing more buttons to make it stop. They only made things worse as the skateboard swerved in all directions.

"Ahhhhh!" Chet screamed as the board headed toward the playground.

"Why doesn't he just jump off?" Joe asked.

"He's probably scared," Frank replied as they ran.

"Speaking of scary," Joe groaned. "Look who's back."

Both brothers slowed down as Adam, Seth, Tony, and Diesel charged over, ice-cream treats in their hands.

"Give me that remote," Adam ordered. He grabbed the device from Joe's hand and flicked a switch. All eyes turned to Chet as the skateboard screeched to a stop.

"Whooaaa!" Chet cried as he flew off the skateboard into the sandbox with a loud *PLOOF*!

"Let's see if he's okay!" Frank told Joe.

The brothers ran to the sandbox to help Chet. Adam and his friends raced straight to the skateboard.

"No big kids allowed!" a three-year-old girl scolded Chet as he lay sprawled in the sand.

Before Frank and Joe could step into the sandbox, they were surrounded by the bullies.

"Stealing Diesel's skateboard?" Adam sneered as he held his drippy chocolate ice-cream bar over Joe's head. "Sour grapes because your tuna-breath cat's a big loser?"

Joe's gritted his teeth as ice cream dripped on his head and down his forehead. Suddenly—

"I'm afraid you're the loser, kid," a man's voice spoke up.

All eyes turned to see Lou Simonetti. The owner of the Easy Cheesy truck was walking over with a frown.

"I heard and saw everything," Lou said. "And electronic skateboards were against the rules of today's contest."

"Against the rules?" Diesel asked through a mouthful of coconut crunch. "Who says?"

"The rules say," Lou replied. "Didn't you read them before you signed up for the contest?"

"Yeah, didn't you . . . Champ?" Chet said, flicking sand off his shoulder in Diesel's direction.

"I hate to tell you this, Diesel," Lou said. "But you'll have to give up your title and prizes to the runner-up, Felicia Singh."

"What?" Diesel exclaimed. "No way!"

"Diesel won fair and square!" Adam argued.

"He won," Lou said, raising an eyebrow. "But not fairly."

The brothers and Chet traded grins. Adam might not have run the mechanical mouse, but he was caught remote-handed!

"Your trick may have worked, Ackerman," Joe stated, "but now the joke's on you!"

Adam glared at Joe, but not for long. Lou wanted answers, and he wanted them now!

"We'll be going now," Chet said with a little wave to the bullies. "Have a nice day!"

"Are you okay after that crazy ride, Chet?" Joe asked.

"Nothing that a fudge pop can't help!" Chet said. "I'll catch up with you guys later."

Chet left for the ice-cream cart. Joe opened his clue book and crossed Adam's name off his suspect list.

"Adam's not guilty," he said. "Sneaky, but not guilty."

"Let's move on to our next suspect," Frank suggested. "That would be Phil."

"I told you, Frank," Joe said, shaking his head. "I don't think Phil would do anything bad to Skeeter." He closed his clue book and added, "Besides, Dad always says not to accuse anyone unless we have enough evidence or clues."

"So let's look for clues at the scene of the crime," Frank agreed. "Give me the clue book. There's something I want to figure out."

Joe followed Frank back to where the skateboard contest had been. The starting point was still chalked on the ground—the same spot where Skeeter had seen the mouse.

"The mouse was heading in that direction," Frank explained, pointing to the bushes where they'd found the mouse, "which means it probably came from the opposite direction."

Frank knew which way the mouse had come from, but he couldn't resist doodling in the clue book. On a fresh page he drew an *X* to mark where Skeeter saw the mouse. He then drew two straight arrows going in opposite directions.

Frank and Joe turned to see where the mouse had come from. It was another clump of bushes. They squeezed through the bushes and found themselves in a small clearing.

"Look!" Joe said, pointing at two long, skinny track marks in the dirt. "Those tracks lead from here out of the bushes."

Joe pulled the mechanical mouse from his pocket. He compared the wheels underneath the mouse to the track marks on the ground.

"They're a perfect match," Joe pointed out. "Too bad the tracks don't tell us who ran the mouse in the first place."

"Oh, yeah?" Frank said. "Check that out!"

Joe looked to see where Frank was pointing. Sticking out from underneath a bush was a dark-red Frisbee covered with brown polka dots.

"Uh-oh," Joe muttered under his breath.

Frisbee . . . Frisbee-catching dog . . . Phil!

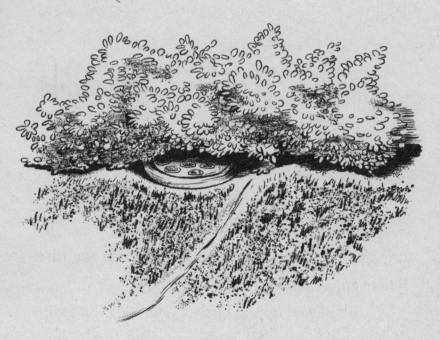

Chapter
7

REMOTELY IMPOSSIBLE

"Phil's dog does catch Frisbees," Frank admitted.

"But if Phil and Champ were back here," Joe argued, "wouldn't there be paw prints in the dirt? There are none!"

Frank picked up the Frisbee and said, "Red with brown polka dots. What a weird color combo for a Frisbee."

Joe knew the arrows were starting to point to Phil. But he still hated writing his friend's name on the suspect list. "I guess next we have to question Phil," he sighed.

"Let's do that tomorrow," Frank decided. "It's getting late. Plus, you have chocolate ice cream in your hair."

Joe ran his hand through his sticky hair. "Then I'd better wash it out," he agreed. "Mom and Dad said we might go out for dinner. I'm hoping it's Leaning Tower of Pizza or Pizza Prince."

"We usually go for burgers Saturday nights," Frank said.

"I can't explain it, Frank," Joe explained, "but I suddenly have this weird craving for pizza with pepperoni!"

"As long as it's not mac and cheese," Frank groaned. "I am so over that for now!"

It was Joe's lucky night. The Hardys shared a booth and two pies at Pizza Prince. One pie was pepperoni!

"This place is packed tonight," Frank said.

"Yeah!" Joe said, shaking extra cheese on his slice. "Daisy must be happy about that."

"No one looks happier than Matty and Scotty," Frank said. He nodded toward the twins in the corner of the restaurant. The boys were laughing and watching a cartoon on the hanging TV monitor.

"Say, Joe?" Mr. Hardy asked, pointing to the mechanical mouse on the table. "Did you have to bring that thing?"

"Dad, I bring my clue book wherever I go," Joe said with a smile. "So why not my clues?"

"Because that one happens to be gross," Mrs. Hardy said.

"Don't worry, Mom," Frank assured her. "We don't have the remote that goes with it."

"Without the remote, that mouse isn't going anywhere!" Joe added. He was about to continue eating when—

WHIRRRRRRRRR!!

Everyone's hands froze on their pizza slices. The once-still mechanical mouse had begun spinning around and around on the table!

"Holy macaroni!" Joe exclaimed.

"How did that happen?" cried Frank.

"Boys, please make it stop," their mother insisted as the mouse started whizzing across the table. "It just knocked over the oregano!"

"That's just it, Mom!" Frank said. "Without the remote, we can't make it do anything!"

"Here's one way," said Mr. Hardy. He was about to grab the mouse when it came to a stop.

Joe looked to see the other customers staring at them. Even Matty and Scotty turned from their cartoon to gawk.

"Guys, are you sure that thing doesn't run on batteries?" Mr. Hardy asked.

Joe flipped the mouse over to show no battery compartment. "See, Dad?" he said. "You control it with a remote."

"Which means," Frank said, leaning forward, "someone in this pizza place has the missing remote."

Suddenly—

"Hey, Frank. Hi, Joe," a voice said. "Cool mouse."

Frank and Joe looked up. It was Phil!

"Today was awesome, you guys," Phil called back as he followed his parents to a table. "Champ is still the number one pet in Bayport!"

Chapter 8

FETCHING FIND

"Did you hear what Phil just said about Champ?" Joe asked Frank when Phil was out of earshot. "I didn't want to think it—but maybe he did sabotage Skeeter."

"We didn't see Phil at the skateboard contest," Frank said, "but if he has the remote, he's the one who just moved the mouse!"

"His mouse!" Joe added. "Let's ask him some questions before he goes home."

But as Frank and Joe began standing, Mrs. Hardy shook her head.

"I don't think so," their mother said. "We have a rule, remember?"

"No case should ever interrupt dinner," Mr. Hardy reminded the brothers.

"But Dad, you're a private investigator," Joe said. "What would you do?"

"Well, I wouldn't want to accuse a good friend," their father admitted. "It's a tough call, guys."

"That's for sure," Joe sighed before picking up his slice, "but we have to find that remote."

The next morning couldn't come fast enough for Frank and Joe. After eating breakfast, they headed straight to the Cohen house.

"Hi, guys," Mrs. Cohen said after opening the door. "Phil just left to walk Champ around the block."

"Mrs. Cohen? Phil told us that yesterday was an awesome day for Champ," Frank said. "What did he mean?"

"Oh, Phil meant that Champ held on to his title as number one pet star in Bayport," Mrs. Cohen said proudly.

"How did he do that?" Joe asked, thinking about the mechanical mouse.

Before Mrs. Cohen could answer, her cell phone rang. She told the caller to hold, then said to the boys, "Why don't you wait for Phil in his room? There are lots of things up there to keep you busy."

Mrs. Cohen opened the door wide to let the brothers inside. She then turned back to her call.

"Lots of clues to keep us busy, I hope," Frank whispered to Joe as they made their way upstairs.

"This can't be hard, Frank," Joe said when they reached the second-floor landing. "All we have to do is look for the remote that goes with the mouse."

But when the boys entered Phil's room, they froze. They'd forgotten how many remotes he had— and how many gadgets!

"Frank, check that out!" Joe said, pointing to a miniature black helicopter on Phil's worktable. "I wonder how it works."

"Forget that," Frank said. "Where do we start with all these remotes?"

"There's only one way to start," Joe said. "We have to test all the remotes until we find the one that works the mouse."

"No way," said Frank, shaking his head. "Remember what happened when we tested the skateboard remote?"

"Chet went flying," Joe sighed. "Got it."

As they looked around the room, Joe's eyes fell on a shiny gold trophy on Phil's desk. The trophy was a statue of a dog with a Frisbee in his mouth.

Joe read the words engraved on the base of the trophy: "'First Prize, Fido Fris-bee Fetch Tournament.'"

"So?" Frank said. He pointed to more dog-shaped trophies on one of Phil's shelves. "Champ has won lots of trophies for catching Frisbees."

"But I bet he won this trophy yesterday," Joe stated.

"And if Phil took Champ to the Frisbee Fetch yesterday, he couldn't have been at the skateboarding contest."

"What makes you think it was yesterday?" Frank asked. "Is there a date on the plaque?"

"No," Joe said. "But this trophy is super shiny, like most new trophies. Plus, it's on Phil's desk, not with his other trophies on the shelf."

"Okay," Frank agreed. "But that still doesn't tell us when that tournament was held."

As Joe put back the trophy, he noticed Phil's computer, open to YouTube.

"Phil puts all of Champ's Frisbee-catching videos on YouTube," Joe said. "There's the video from the Fido Fetch tournament!"

Joe leaned closer to read the description. He smiled and said, "The date of the Fido Fetch was yesterday, Frank!"

As Frank studied the video, he noticed something too. "The tournament was held at the Bayport Athletic Field," he pointed out. "There's the clock tower."

Joe enlarged the video full-screen to read the clock.

"The time is eleven o'clock!" he stated. "That's the time the skateboard contest started—which means Phil couldn't have been there to trick Skeeter."

"The Fido Fetch is Phil's alibi!" Frank said, happy to rule out their friend.

"And that means none of these remotes belong to our mechanical mouse!" Joe declared. He held one up to make a point when—

"Woof, woof!" Champ barked as he ran into the room.

The bulldog jumped up on Joe, making him drop the remote.

As the remote clattered on the floor, a strange whirring noise rose from the other side of the room. The boys turned to see the black helicopter rise toward the ceiling—then take off around the room.

"It's a drone!" Frank cried out.

"And it's spraying water!" shouted Joe.

Champ yipped and the brothers yelped as the water-copter drone swooped down to drench them even more!

"Duck, Frank, duck!" Joe screamed. "We're under attack!!"

Chapter 9

PIZZA PIE SPY

"What the—hey?" Phil cried as he ran into the room. He caught up with Champ darting around the room with the remote between his teeth.

Phil held out his hand under Champ's mouth. "That's not a Frisbee! Drop it! Drop it!"

Frank and Joe had run for shelter underneath Phil's worktable. They peeked out to see the sad-eyed bulldog drop the remote on the floor with a *clunk*.

Grabbing the remote, Phil flicked a switch. The

copter sputtered in the air before descending gently onto Phil's desk.

"What was that thing, Phil?" Frank demanded as the brothers slipped out from underneath the table.

"My latest invention," Phil explained. "The copter waters your lawn so you don't have to. But I didn't test it yet."

"Um . . . I think you just did," Joe said shaking out his wet hair. "And it works."

Puzzled, Phil looked from Joe to Frank. "What were you guys doing in my room, anyway?" he asked.

"Your mom told us we could wait up here for you," Frank explained. "But we were also working on a new case."

"What case?" Phil asked.

Joe held up the mechanical mouse. "Someone ran this past Skeeter at the skateboard contest," he explained. "Frank and I are trying to figure out who did it."

"That's the fake mouse you had at the pizza place last night!" Phil said. "Why do you think it was mine?"

"We thought maybe you built a mechanical

mouse to get Skeeter out of the contest," Joe admitted. "But now we know you didn't."

Phil rolled his eyes. "Yeah, duh!" he said. "I build gadgets for fun—not to mess with cats!"

"Sorry, Phil," Frank admitted. "We didn't want to suspect you, but we have to follow all our leads."

"We're detectives," Joe said with a smile. "That's how we roll."

"It's all good," Phil said, smiling too. "Champ proved yesterday he's still the number one pet star in Bayport."

Phil walked over to his computer and pointed to Champ's video. "See?" he said excitedly. "Over ten thousand likes!"

"Way to go, Champ," Joe said, giving the bulldog a pat. "And speaking of Frisbees, we found one in the park yesterday."

"A red Frisbee with brown polka dots," added Frank. "Was it Champ's?"

"Red with brown polka dots is a weird color for a Frisbee," Phil said. "And it wasn't Champ's. He never chased a Frisbee he didn't catch."

Frank and Joe were happy Phil wasn't guilty. They were also happy for Champ—still top dog in Bayport!

"We can help you mop up these puddles, Phil," Joe said, nodding down at the wet floor.

"Thanks, but no thanks," Phil said. "As long as the puddles weren't made by Champ, I can deal with it."

Champ jutted out his lower lip and rolled his eyes as if to say, *Very funny.*

After saying good-bye to the Cohens, the brothers left to continue their case. But there wasn't much case to continue.

"No more suspects, Frank," Joe said as he crossed Phil's name from the suspect list. "What now?"

"Let's go back to the park and look for more

clues," Frank decided. "Somebody was behind those bushes where the mouse was launched."

"Yeah," Joe said as he shut his clue book. "Somebody we haven't figured out yet."

The brothers returned to the park and the scene of the crime. As they stood behind the bushes, Frank said, "Okay. What do we know so far?"

Joe pointed to the ground and said, "We know that's where we found that funny-looking red Frisbee with brown polka dots."

"The one that looks more like a pizza than a Frisbee!" Frank joked.

Pizza? Joe stared at Frank.

"The Frisbee looks like a pepperoni pizza!" Joe exclaimed. "Frank, no wonder I had a weird craving for some after we found the Frisbee."

"Okay," Frank said with a shrug. "Now let's go back to the case—"

"Frank, Daisy told us Pizza Palace was giving away free Frisbees with every pizza delivery," Joe cut in excitedly. "So it does have something to do with the case. A lot of something!"

THE HARDY BOYS—and
YOU!

CAN YOU SOLVE THE MYSTERY OF THE SKATEBOARD SABOTEUR?

Try thinking like Frank and Joe or turn the page to find out!

1. Frank and Joe ruled out Aunt Trudy, Adam, and Phil. Can you think of other suspects? Write them down on a piece of paper.

2. What happened at the Leaning Tower of Pizza that could make the pepperoni Frisbee a clue? Write down your ideas on a piece of paper.

3. The Hardys' friend Phil likes to invent gadgets. What gadgets might he invent to help Frank and Joe solve mysteries? Write your ideas on a piece of paper.

Chapter 10

DOUBLE TROUBLE

Frank narrowed his eyes thoughtfully. "Come to think of it," he said, "the pizza place is where the mouse went crazy last night."

"Someone at the pizza place had the remote for the mouse," Joe explained. "Someone who could have worked there!"

"You mean Daisy Zamora?" Frank asked.

The sound of a snapping twig made the brothers jump. They turned to see Matty and Scotty Zamora on the other side of the bushes. They seemed to be standing on their toes, staring over the hedge straight at Frank and Joe.

"What are you doing here?" Joe asked.

"We came to look for our Frisbee," Matty answered. "Instead we found you."

Frank and Joe exchanged glances. The Frisbee had belonged to the twins. And they'd been in the pizza place last night!

"We did find a Frisbee," Joe said. "We also found this." He pulled the fake mouse from his pocket. "Anybody know where we can find the remote that goes with it?"

Matty and Scotty didn't answer. Instead they turned and took off.

"Come on, Frank!" Joe said. "Let's get those twins!"

Frank and Joe jumped over the bushes.

"They're running into the playground!" Frank shouted as they chased the twins.

"Then we're running in there too!" Joe shouted back.

Matty and Scotty ran past the swings and see-saws to the challenge course. The colorful course was filled with ropes, tunnels, planks, and hoops.

In a flash, Matty and Scotty charged through the course. So did Frank and Joe. They chased the twins across a high plank, crawled after them through a tunnel —even stepped in and out of tires in hot pursuit.

"I didn't know pizza was energy food!" Joe shouted to Frank as the twins took the lead.

Matty and Scotty had climbed a rope ladder leading to a long, winding tunnel slide. Joe was about to climb after them when Frank said, "Let's surprise them down here."

Their arms folded, Frank and Joe waited by the mouth of the tunnel.

A loud "Wheeeeeee" echoed inside the tunnel. Then out popped Matty, feet first.

Matty gulped when he saw Frank and Joe.

"Okay, Scotty," Joe yelled up the tunnel. "Come out, come out, wherever you are!"

Instead of Scotty, out slid a silver gadget with buttons!

"A remote!" Frank exclaimed.

"It must have fallen out of Scotty's pocket," Joe said excitedly. "Are we lucky or what?"

Joe grabbed the remote just as Scotty burst through the tunnel, headfirst. When Scotty saw the remote in Joe's hand, he mumbled, "Oops."

Frank and Joe tested the remote with the mechanical mouse. The mouse began spinning around, and they high-fived!

"You had to slide upside down," Matty complained to Scotty. "Show-off!"

Frank clicked the remote to stop the mouse. "So you guys moved the mouse last night in the pizza place, right?" he asked the twins.

"Yes, but we didn't mean to!" Matty insisted.

"Our dad told us our cartoon was too loud," Scotty explained. "So we used the remote to make it not so loud."

"Except Scotty used the wrong remote," Matty sighed. "He used the one for the fake mouse."

"It was on the table," Scotty said, his eyes cast downward. "I took it out of my pocket before, when I was looking for my gum."

"It's the same mouse that Skeeter chased at the skateboarding contest," Joe said with a frown. "Why did you want to ruin Skeeter's big chance?"

Matty shook his head. "We didn't want to ruin Skeeter!" he insisted. "We wanted to ruin Easy Cheesy!"

"Easy Cheesy?" Joe asked, wrinkling his nose.

"The macaroni-and-cheese truck?" Frank asked. "What do you have against them?"

Scotty dug his sneaker toe into the dirt as he explained, "Daisy said if more people ate macaroni and cheese than pizza, then Pizza Prince would close down."

"But if people saw a mouse running by the tables," Scotty said, "they wouldn't want to eat there ever again!"

"We told Daisy we were going to play Frisbee," Matty explained. "Instead we hid behind the bushes and aimed the mouse straight for the tables. Except it didn't go straight."

"It hit a rock and spun around," Scotty went on, his eyes wide. "Then the fake mouse zoomed toward Skeeter!"

"We didn't know Skeeter would chase the mouse," Matty sighed. "But our plan still worked."

"Everybody saw the mouse," Scotty continued. "And now business at Pizza Prince is booming."

"Ka-booming," Matty added, looking unhappy.

Frank and Joe noticed the twins' sad faces. What was up with that?

"If your plan worked," Frank said slowly, "why do you look so sad?"

"Ever since our pizza place got so busy," Scotty explained, "so did our mom and dad."

"All they've been doing since then is work, work, work!" Matty complained. He held out his hand and said, "Can we have our mouse back?"

Joe handed back the mouse and the remote. Matty and Scotty mumbled, "Thanks," then walked away.

"I kind of feel bad for the twins," Frank admitted. "But glad that we found out who tricked Skeeter."

"Now we can tell Carlos the fake mouse was nothing personal," Joe said.

"It was personal for Lou," Frank said, nodding toward the Easy Cheesy Mac and Cheese truck. "Thanks to that mouse, he lost half his customers."

"I wish there was a way to bring customers back to Easy Cheesy," Joe said, gazing at the almost-empty café tables. "But what?"

Suddenly—"Arrrrrk!"

Joe gasped as a huge red-and-green parrot flew out of nowhere to land on his shoulder.

"Where did he come from?" Frank asked.

"I wonder if he talks," Joe said.

The parrot squawked, rolled his head, and began to sing: "I've got spuuuuurs that jingle jangle jiiiingle!"

"He doesn't just talk," Joe laughed, "he sings!"

"You found my parrot!"

The brothers turned to see Jason Wang from school hurrying over. He held out his wrist for the parrot to hop on.

"Does your parrot always sing?" Joe asked.

"He knows seven tunes!" Jason said proudly. "Who needs to download music when you have Crackers!"

"You should be daaaaancing!" Crackers squawked. "Arrrk!"

"Wow, Joe," Frank said as Jason carried Crackers away. "Bayport has some crazy-talented pets."

Talented? Pets? Joe's eyes lit up.

"Frank, that's it!" he exclaimed. "That's how we can bring customers back to Easy Cheesy."

"How?" Frank asked.

"With a talent show just for pets!" Joe exclaimed. "It can be held in the park right by the Easy Cheesy Mac and Cheese truck."

Joe watched as his brother thought it over. "What do you think, Frank?" he asked.

"I think as long as those pets aren't mice," Frank teased, "a cool show like that could solve Lou's problem."

"We solved something too, Frank," Joe said with a smile as he wrote *Case Closed* in his clue book. "Another mystery!"

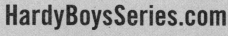
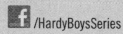

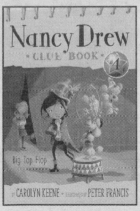